Salome

DOVER·THRIFT·EDITIONS

Salome

OSCAR WILDE

DOVER PUBLICATIONS, INC.
Mineola, New York

DOVER THRIFT EDITIONS

GENERAL EDITOR: PAUL NEGRI
EDITOR OF THIS VOLUME: JOSLYN T. PINE

Published in Canada by General Publishing Company, Ltd., 895 Don Mills Road, 400-2 Park Centre, Toronto, Ontario M3C 1W3.

Published in the United Kingdom by David & Charles, Brunel House, Forde Close, Newton Abbot, Devon TQ12 4PU.

Theatrical Rights

This Dover Thrift Edition may be used in its entirety, in adaptation, or in any other way for theatrical productions, professional and amateur, in the United States, without fee, permission, or acknowledgment. (This may not apply outside of the United States, as copyright conditions may vary.)

Bibliographical Note

This Dover edition, first published in 2002, is an unabridged republication of the text of the first English edition of *Salome*, published in 1894 by Elkin Mathews & John Lane, London. The introductory essay, "A Note on *Salome*," was written by Robert Ross for the 1930 edition of *Salome* published by John Lane, The Bodley Head, London.

Library of Congress Cataloging-in-Publication Data

Wilde, Oscar, 1854–1900.
   [Salomé. English]
   Salome / Oscar Wilde.
     p. cm. — (Dover thrift editions)
   "Unabridged republication of the text of the first English edition"—T.p. verso.
   "The introductory essay, 'A note on Salome,' was written by Robert Ross for the 1930 edition . . . published by John Lane, The Bodley Head, London"—T.p. verso.
   ISBN 0-486-42127-9 (pbk.)
   1. Salome (Biblical figure)—Drama. I. Title. II. Series.

PR5820.S2 E5 2002
822'.8—dc21

2001050838

Manufactured in the United States of America
Dover Publications, Inc., 31 East 2nd Street, Mineola, N.Y. 11501

A Note on *Salome**

Salome has made the author's name a household word wherever the English language is not spoken. Few English plays have such a peculiar history. Written in French in 1892 it was in full rehearsal by Madame Bernhardt at the Palace Theatre when it was prohibited by the Censor. Oscar Wilde immediately announced his intention of changing his nationality, a characteristic jest, which was only taken seriously, oddly enough, in Ireland. The interference of the Censor has seldom been more popular or more heartily endorsed by English critics. On its publication in book form *Salome* was greeted by a chorus of ridicule, and it may be noted in passing that at least two of the more violent reviews were from the pens of unsuccessful dramatists, while all those whose French never went beyond Ollendorff were glad to find in that venerable school classic an unsuspected asset in their education — a handy missile with which to pelt *Salome* and its author. The correctness of the French was, of course, impugned, although the script had been passed by a distinguished French writer, to whom I have heard the whole work attributed. The *Times*, while depreciating the drama, gave its author credit for a *tour de force*, in being capable of writing a French play for Madame Bernhardt, and this drew from him the following letter: —

*[The author of this Note, Robert Ross, was a lifelong friend of Oscar Wilde as well as his literary executor. The Note originally appeared in the 1930 edition of *Salome* published in London. — PUB.]

The *Times*, Thursday, March 2, 1893, p. 4.

Mr. Oscar Wilde on "SALOME"

To the Editor of The Times.

SIR, *My attention has been drawn to a review of "Salome" which was published in your columns last week. The opinions of English critics on a French work of mine have, of course, little, if any, interest for me. I write simply to ask you to allow me to correct a misstatement that appears in the review in question.*

The fact that the greatest tragic actress of any stage now living saw in my play such beauty that she was anxious to produce it, to take herself the part of the heroine, to lend to the entire poem the glamour of her personality, and to my prose the music of her flute-like voice—this was naturally, and always will be, a source of pride and pleasure to me, and I look forward with delight to seeing Mme. Bernhardt present my play in Paris, that vivid centre of art, where religious dramas are often performed. But my play was in no sense of the words written for this great actress. I have never written a play for any actor or actress, nor shall I ever do so. Such work is for the artisan in literature—not for the artist.

　　I remain, Sir, your obedient servant,

OSCAR WILDE.

When *Salome* was translated into English by Lord Alfred Douglas, the illustrator, Aubrey Beardsley, shared some of the obloquy heaped on Wilde. It is interesting that he should have found inspiration for his finest work in a play he never admired and by a writer he cordially disliked. The motives are, of course, made to his hand, and never was there a more suitable material for that odd tangent art in which there are no tactile values. The amusing caricatures of Wilde which appear in the *Frontispiece*, "Enter Herodias" and "The Eyes of Herod,"* are the only pieces of *vraisemblance* in these exquisite designs. The colophon is a real masterpiece and a witty criticism of the play as well.†

On the production of *Salome* by the New Stage Club in May,

---

*[Also in "A Platonic Lament."—PUB.]

†[This Dover Thrift edition does not include Beardsley's illustration. However, the 1894 illustrated version is available in another Dover reprint of *Salome* (0-486-21830-9).—PUB.]

1905,* the dramatic critics again expressed themselves vehemently, vociferating their regrets that the play had been dragged from its obscurity. The *obscure* drama, however, had become for five years past part of the literature of Europe. It is performed regularly or intermittently in Holland, Sweden, Italy, France, and Russia, and it has been translated into every European language, including the Czech. It forms part of the repertoire of the German stage, where it is performed more often than any play by any English writer except Shakespeare. Owing, perhaps, to what I must call its *obscure* popularity in the continental theatres, Dr. Strauss was preparing his remarkable opera at the very moment when there appeared the criticisms to which I refer, and since the production of the opera in Dresden in December, 1905, English musical journalists and correspondents always refer to the work as *founded* on Wilde's drama. That is the only way in which they can evade an awkward truth—a palpable contravention to their own wishes and theories. The music, however, has been set to the actual words of *Salome* in Madame Hedwig Lachmann's admirable translation. The words have not been transfigured into ordinary operatic nonsense to suit the score, or the susceptibilities of the English people. I observe that admirers of Dr. Strauss are a little mortified that the great master should have found an occasion for composition in a play which they long ago consigned to oblivion and the shambles of Aubrey Beardsley. Wilde himself, in a rhetorical period, seems to have contemplated the possibility of his prose drama for a musical theme. In "De Profundis" he says: "The refrains, whose recurring motifs make 'Salome' so like a piece of music, and bind it together as a ballad."

He was still incarcerated in 1896, when Mons. Luigne Poë† produced the play for the first time at the Théâtre Libre in Paris, with Lina Muntz in the title role. A rather pathetic reference to this occasion occurs in a letter Wilde wrote to me from Reading:—

---

*A more recent performance of *Salome* (1906), by the Literary Theatre Club, has again produced an ebullition of rancour and deliberate misrepresentation on the part of the dramatic critics, the majority of whom are anxious to parade their ignorance of the continental stage. The production was remarkable on account of the beautiful dresses and mounting, for which Mr. Charles Ricketts was responsible, and the marvellous impersonation of Herod by Mr. Robert Farquharson. Wilde used to say that *Salome* was a mirror in which everyone could see himself. The artist, art; the dull, dulness; the vulgar, vulgarity.—R.R.

†[Aurélien François Lugné-Poë, 1869–1940.—PUB.]

"Please say how gratified I was at the performance of my play, and have my thanks conveyed to Luigne Poë. It is something that at a time of disgrace and shame I should still be regarded as an artist. I wish I could feel more pleasure, but I seem dead to all emotions except those of anguish and despair. However, please let Luigne Poë know that I am sensible of the honour he has done me. He is a poet himself. Write to me in answer to this, and try and see what Lemaitre, Bauer, and Sarcey* said of 'Salome.'"

The bias of personal friendship precludes me from praising or defending *Salome*, even if it were necessary to do so. Nothing I might say would add to the reputation of its detractors. Its sources are obvious; particularly Flaubert and Maeterlinck, in whose peculiar and original style it is an essay. A critic, for whom I have a greater regard than many of his contemporaries, says that *Salome* is only a catalogue; but a catalogue can be intensely dramatic, as we know when the performance takes place at Christie's; few plays are more exciting than an auction in King Street when the stars are fighting *for* Sisera.

It has been remarked that Wilde confuses Herod the Great (*Mat.* xi. I),[†] Herod Antipas (*Mat.* xiv. 3), and Herod Agrippa (*Acts* xiii), but the confusion is intentional, as in mediæval mystery plays Herod is taken for a type, not an historical character, and the criticism is about as valuable as that of people who laboriously point out the anachronisms in Beardsley's designs. With reference to the charge of plagiarism brought against *Salome* and its author, I venture to mention a personal recollection.

Wilde complained to me one day that someone in a well-known novel had stolen an idea of his. I pleaded in defence of the culprit that Wilde himself was a fearless literary thief. "My dear friend," he said, with his usual drawling emphasis, "when I see a monstrous tulip with *four* wonderful petals in someone else's garden, I am impelled to grow a monstrous tulip with *five* wonderful petals, but that is no reason why someone should grow a tulip with only *three* petals." THAT WAS OSCAR WILDE.

ROBERT ROSS

---

*[Jules Lemaitre, 1853–1914; Francisque Sarcey, 1828–1899; drama critics.—PUB.]
†[Matthew ii, I.—PUB.]

Salome

The Persons of the Play

HEROD ANTIPAS, TETRARCH OF JUDÆA

IOKANAAN, THE PROPHET

THE YOUNG SYRIAN, CAPTAIN OF THE GUARD

TIGELLINUS, A YOUNG ROMAN

A CAPPADOCIAN

A NUBIAN

FIRST SOLDIER

SECOND SOLDIER

THE PAGE OF HERODIAS

JEWS, NAZARENES, ETC.

A SLAVE

NAAMAN, THE EXECUTIONER

HERODIAS, WIFE OF THE TETRARCH

SALOME, DAUGHTER OF HERODIAS

THE SLAVES OF SALOME

SCENE—*A great terrace in the Palace of Herod, set above the banqueting-hall. Some soldiers are leaning over the balcony. To the right there is a gigantic staircase, to the left, at the back, an old cistern surrounded by a wall of green bronze. The moon is shining very brightly.*

THE YOUNG SYRIAN:
How beautiful is the Princess Salome tonight!

THE PAGE OF HERODIAS:
Look at the moon. How strange the moon seems! She is like a woman rising from a tomb. She is like a dead woman. One might fancy she was looking for dead things.

THE YOUNG SYRIAN:
She has a strange look. She is like a little princess who wears a yellow veil, and whose feet are of silver. She is like a princess who has little white doves for feet. One might fancy she was dancing.

THE PAGE OF HERODIAS:
She is like a woman who is dead. She moves very slowly. [*Noise in the banqueting-hall.*]

FIRST SOLDIER:
What an uproar! Who are those wild beasts howling?

SECOND SOLDIER:
The Jews. They are always like that. They are disputing about their religion.

FIRST SOLDIER:
Why do they dispute about their religion?

3

SECOND SOLDIER:

I cannot tell. They are always doing it. The Pharisees, for instance, say that there are angels, and the Sadducees declare that angels do not exist.

FIRST SOLDIER:

I think it is ridiculous to dispute about such things.

THE YOUNG SYRIAN:

How beautiful is the Princess Salome tonight!

THE PAGE OF HERODIAS:

You are always looking at her. You look at her too much. It is dangerous to look at people in such fashion. Something terrible may happen.

THE YOUNG SYRIAN:

She is very beautiful tonight.

FIRST SOLDIER:

The Tetrarch has a sombre aspect.

SECOND SOLDIER:

Yes; he has a sombre aspect.

FIRST SOLDIER:

He is looking at something.

SECOND SOLDIER:

He is looking at some one.

FIRST SOLDIER:

At whom is he looking?

SECOND SOLDIER:

I cannot tell.

THE YOUNG SYRIAN:

How pale the Princess is! Never have I seen her so pale. She is like the shadow of a white rose in a mirror of silver.

THE PAGE OF HERODIAS:

You must not look at her. You look too much at her.

FIRST SOLDIER:

Herodias has filled the cup of the Tetrarch.

THE CAPPADOCIAN:

Is that the Queen Herodias, she who wears a black mitre sewed with pearls, and whose hair is powdered with blue dust?

FIRST SOLDIER:

Yes; that is Herodias, the Tetrarch's wife.

SECOND SOLDIER:

The Tetrarch is very fond of wine. He has wine of three sorts. One which is brought from the Island of Samothrace, and is purple like the cloak of Cæsar.

THE CAPPADOCIAN:

I have never seen Cæsar.

SECOND SOLDIER:

Another that comes from a town called Cyprus, and is as yellow as gold.

THE CAPPADOCIAN:

I love gold.

SECOND SOLDIER:

And the third is a wine of Sicily. That wine is as red as blood.

THE NUBIAN:

The gods of my country are very fond of blood. Twice in the year we sacrifice to them young men and maidens: fifty young men and a hundred maidens. But I am afraid that we never give them quite enough, for they are very harsh to us.

THE CAPPADOCIAN:

In my country there are no gods left. The Romans have driven them out. There are some who say that they have hidden themselves in the mountains, but I do not believe it. Three nights I have been on the mountains seeking them everywhere. I did not find them, and at last I called them by their names, and they did not come. I think they are dead.

FIRST SOLDIER:
The Jews worship a God that one cannot see.

THE CAPPADOCIAN:
I cannot understand that.

FIRST SOLDIER:
In fact, they only believe in things that one cannot see.

THE CAPPADOCIAN:
That seems to me altogether ridiculous.

THE VOICE OF IOKANAAN:
After me shall come another mightier than I. I am not worthy so much as to unloose the latchet of his shoes. When he cometh the solitary places shall be glad. They shall blossom like the rose. The eyes of the blind shall see the day, and the ears of the deaf shall be opened. The sucking child shall put his hand upon the dragon's lair, he shall lead the lions by their manes.

SECOND SOLDIER:
Make him be silent. He is always saying ridiculous things.

FIRST SOLDIER:
No, no. He is a holy man. He is very gentle, too. Every day when I give him to eat he thanks me.

THE CAPPADOCIAN:
Who is he?

FIRST SOLDIER:
A prophet.

THE CAPPADOCIAN:
What is his name?

FIRST SOLDIER:
Iokanaan.

THE CAPPADOCIAN:
Whence comes he?

FIRST SOLDIER:
From the desert, where he fed on locusts and wild honey. He

was clothed in camel's hair, and round his loins he had a leathern belt. He was very terrible to look upon. A great multitude used to follow him. He even had disciples.

THE CAPPADOCIAN:
What is he talking of?

FIRST SOLDIER:
We can never tell. Sometimes he says things that affright one, but it is impossible to understand what he says.

THE CAPPADOCIAN:
May one see him?

FIRST SOLDIER:
No. The Tetrarch has forbidden it.

THE YOUNG SYRIAN:
The Princess has hidden her face behind her fan! Her little white hands are fluttering like doves that fly to their dove-cots. They are like white butterflies. They are just like white butterflies.

THE PAGE OF HERODIAS:
What is that to you? Why do you look at her? You must not look at her. . . . Something terrible may happen.

THE CAPPADOCIAN:
[*Pointing to the cistern.*] What a strange prison!

SECOND SOLDIER:
It is an old cistern.

THE CAPPADOCIAN:
An old cistern! That must be a poisonous place in which to dwell!

SECOND SOLDIER:
Oh no! For instance, the Tetrarch's brother, his elder brother, the first husband of Herodias the Queen, was imprisoned there for twelve years. It did not kill him. At the end of the twelve years he had to be strangled.

THE CAPPADOCIAN:
Strangled? Who dared to do that?

SECOND SOLDIER:
[*Pointing to the Executioner, a huge negro.*] That man yonder, Naaman.

THE CAPPADOCIAN:
He was not afraid?

SECOND SOLDIER:
Oh no! The Tetrarch sent him the ring.

THE CAPPADOCIAN:
What ring?

SECOND SOLDIER:
The death ring. So he was not afraid.

THE CAPPADOCIAN:
Yet it is a terrible thing to strangle a king.

FIRST SOLDIER:
Why? Kings have but one neck, like other men.

THE CAPPADOCIAN:
I think it terrible.

THE YOUNG SYRIAN:
The Princess is getting up! She is leaving the table! She looks very troubled. Ah, she is coming this way. Yes, she is coming towards us. How pale she is! Never have I seen her so pale.

THE PAGE OF HERODIAS:
Do not look at her. I pray you not to look at her.

THE YOUNG SYRIAN:
She is like a dove that has strayed. . . . She is like a narcissus trembling in the wind. . . . She is like a silver flower. [*Enter Salome.*]

SALOME:
I will not stay. I cannot stay. Why does the Tetrarch look at me all the while with his mole's eyes under his shaking eyelids? It is strange that the husband of my mother looks at me like that. I know not what it means. Of a truth I know it too well.

THE YOUNG SYRIAN:

You have left the feast, Princess?

SALOME:

How sweet is the air here! I can breathe here! Within there are Jews from Jerusalem who are tearing each other in pieces over their foolish ceremonies, and barbarians who drink and drink and spill their wine on the pavement, and Greeks from Smyrna with painted eyes and painted cheeks, and frizzed hair curled in columns, and Egyptians silent and subtle, with long nails of jade and russet cloaks, and Romans brutal and coarse, with their uncouth jargon. Ah! how I loathe the Romans! They are rough and common, and they give themselves the airs of noble lords.

THE YOUNG SYRIAN:

Will you be seated, Princess.

THE PAGE OF HERODIAS:

Why do you speak to her? Oh! something terrible will happen. Why do you look at her?

SALOME:

How good to see the moon! She is like a little piece of money, a little silver flower. She is cold and chaste. I am sure she is a virgin. She has the beauty of a virgin. Yes, she is a virgin. She has never defiled herself. She has never abandoned herself to men, like the other goddesses.

THE VOICE OF IOKANAAN:

Behold! the Lord hath come. The Son of Man is at hand. The centaurs have hidden themselves in the rivers, and the nymphs have left the rivers, and are lying beneath the leaves in the forests.

SALOME:

Who was that who cried out?

SECOND SOLDIER:

The prophet, Princess.

SALOME:

Ah, the prophet! He of whom the Tetrarch is afraid?

SECOND SOLDIER:
We know nothing of that, Princess. It was the prophet Iokanaan who cried out.

THE YOUNG SYRIAN:
Is it your pleasure that I bid them bring your litter, Princess? The night is fair in the garden.

SALOME:
He says terrible things about my mother, does he not?

SECOND SOLDIER:
We never understand what he says, Princess.

SALOME:
Yes; he says terrible things about her. [*Enter a Slave.*]

THE SLAVE:
Princess, the Tetrarch prays you to return to the feast.

SALOME:
I will not return.

THE YOUNG SYRIAN:
Pardon me, Princess, but if you return not some misfortune may happen.

SALOME:
Is he an old man, this prophet?

THE YOUNG SYRIAN:
Princess, it were better to return. Suffer me to lead you in.

SALOME:
This prophet . . . is he an old man?

FIRST SOLDIER:
No, Princess, he is quite young.

SECOND SOLDIER:
One cannot be sure. There are those who say that he is Elias.

SALOME:
Who is Elias?

SECOND SOLDIER:
  A prophet of this country in bygone days, Princess.

THE SLAVE:
  What answer may I give the Tetrarch from the Princess?

THE VOICE OF IOKANAAN:
  Rejoice not, O land of Palestine, because the rod of him who
smote thee is broken. For from the seed of the serpent shall
come a basilisk, and that which is born of it shall devour the
birds.

SALOME:
  What a strange voice! I would speak with him.

FIRST SOLDIER:
  I fear it may not be, Princess. The Tetrarch does not suffer any
one to speak with him. He has even forbidden the high priest to
speak with him.

SALOME:
  I desire to speak with him.

FIRST SOLDIER:
  It is impossible, Princess.

SALOME:
  I will speak with him.

THE YOUNG SYRIAN:
  Would it not be better to return to the banquet?

SALOME:
  Bring forth this prophet. [*Exit the Slave.*]

FIRST SOLDIER:
  We dare not, Princess.

SALOME:
  [*Approaching the cistern and looking down into it.*] How black
it is, down there! It must be terrible to be in so black a hole! It is
like a tomb. . . . [*To the soldiers.*] Did you not hear me? Bring out
the prophet. I would look on him.

SECOND SOLDIER:
Princess, I beg you, do not require this of us.

SALOME:
You are making me wait upon your pleasure.

FIRST SOLDIER:
Princess, our lives belong to you, but we cannot do what you have asked of us. And indeed, it is not of us that you should ask this thing.

SALOME:
[*Looking at the young Syrian.*] Ah!

THE PAGE OF HERODIAS:
Oh! what is going to happen? I am sure that something terrible will happen.

SALOME:
[*Going up to the young Syrian.*] Thou wilt do this thing for me, wilt thou not, Narraboth? Thou wilt do this thing for me. I have ever been kind towards thee. Thou wilt do it for me. I would but look at him, this strange prophet. Men have talked so much of him. Often I have heard the Tetrarch talk of him. I think he is afraid of him, the Tetrarch. Art thou, even thou, also afraid of him, Narraboth?

THE YOUNG SYRIAN:
I fear him not, Princess; there is no man I fear. But the Tetrarch has formally forbidden that any man should raise the cover of this well.

SALOME:
Thou wilt do this thing for me, Narraboth, and tomorrow when I pass in my litter beneath the gateway of the idol-sellers I will let fall for thee a little flower, a little green flower.

THE YOUNG SYRIAN:
Princess, I cannot, I cannot.

SALOME:
[*Smiling.*] Thou wilt do this thing for me, Narraboth. Thou knowest that thou wilt do this thing for me. And on the morrow

when I shall pass in my litter by the bridge of the idol-buyers, I will look at thee through the muslin veils, I will look at thee, Narraboth, it may be I will smile at thee. Look at me, Narraboth, look at me. Ah! thou knowest that thou wilt do what I ask of thee. Thou knowest it. . . . I know that thou wilt do this thing.

THE YOUNG SYRIAN:

[*Signing to the third Soldier.*] Let the prophet come forth. . . . The Princess Salome desires to see him.

SALOME:

Ah!

THE PAGE OF HERODIAS:

Oh! How strange the moon looks! Like the hand of a dead woman who is seeking to cover herself with a shroud.

THE YOUNG SYRIAN:

She has a strange aspect! She is like a little princess, whose eyes are eyes of amber. Through the clouds of muslin she is smiling like a little princess. [*The prophet comes out of the cistern. Salome looks at him and steps slowly back.*]

IOKANAAN:

Where is he whose cup of abominations is now full? Where is he, who in a robe of silver shall one day die in the face of all the people? Bid him come forth, that he may hear the voice of him who hath cried in the waste places and in the houses of kings.

SALOME:

Of whom is he speaking?

THE YOUNG SYRIAN:

No one can tell, Princess.

IOKANAAN:

Where is she who saw the images of men painted on the walls, even the images of the Chaldæans painted with colours, and gave herself up unto the lust of her eyes, and sent ambassadors into the land of Chaldæa?

SALOME:

It is of my mother that he is speaking.

THE YOUNG SYRIAN:

Oh no, Princess.

SALOME:

Yes: it is of my mother that he is speaking.

IOKANAAN:

Where is she who gave herself unto the Captains of Assyria, who have baldricks on their loins, and crowns of many colours on their heads? Where is she who hath given herself to the young men of the Egyptians, who are clothed in fine linen and hyacinth, whose shields are of gold, whose helmets are of silver, whose bodies are mighty? Go, bid her rise up from the bed of her abominations, from the bed of her incestuousness, that she may hear the words of him who prepareth the way of the Lord, that she may repent her of her iniquities. Though she will not repent, but will stick fast in her abominations, go bid her come, for the fan of the Lord is in His hand.

SALOME:

Ah, but he is terrible, he is terrible!

THE YOUNG SYRIAN:

Do not stay here, Princess, I beseech you.

SALOME:

It is his eyes above all that are terrible. They are like black holes burnt by torches in a tapestry of Tyre. They are like the black caverns where the dragons live, the black caverns of Egypt in which the dragons make their lairs. They are like black lakes troubled by fantastic moons. . . . Do you think he will speak again?

THE YOUNG SYRIAN:

Do not stay here, Princess. I pray you do not stay here.

SALOME:

How wasted he is! He is like a thin ivory statue. He is like an image of silver. I am sure he is chaste, as the moon is. He is like a moonbeam, like a shaft of silver. His flesh must be very cold, cold as ivory. . . . I would look closer at him.

THE YOUNG SYRIAN:
   No, no, Princess!

SALOME:
   I must look at him closer.

THE YOUNG SYRIAN:
   Princess! Princess!

IOKANAAN:
   Who is this woman who is looking at me? I will not have her look at me. Wherefore doth she look at me, with her golden eyes, under her gilded eyelids? I know not who she is. I do not desire to know who she is. Bid her begone. It is not to her that I would speak.

SALOME:
   I am Salome, daughter of Herodias, Princess of Judæa.

IOKANAAN:
   Back! daughter of Babylon! Come not near the chosen of the Lord. Thy mother hath filled the earth with the wine of her iniquities, and the cry of her sinning hath come up even to the ears of God.

SALOME:
   Speak again, Iokanaan. Thy voice is as music to mine ear.

THE YOUNG SYRIAN:
   Princess! Princess! Princess!

SALOME:
   Speak again! Speak again, Iokanaan, and tell me what I must do.

IOKANAAN:
   Daughter of Sodom, come not near me! But cover thy face with a veil, and scatter ashes upon thine head, and get thee to the desert, and seek out the Son of Man.

SALOME:
   Who is he, the Son of Man? Is he as beautiful as thou art, Iokanaan?

IOKANAAN:

Get thee behind me! I hear in the palace the beating of the wings of the angel of death.

THE YOUNG SYRIAN:

Princess, I beseech thee to go within.

IOKANAAN:

Angel of the Lord God, what dost thou here with thy sword? Whom seekest thou in this palace? The day of him who shall die in a robe of silver has not yet come.

SALOME:

Iokanaan!

IOKANAAN:

Who speaketh?

SALOME:

I am amorous of thy body, Iokanaan! Thy body is white, like the lilies of a field that the mower hath never mowed. Thy body is white like the snows that lie on the mountains of Judæa, and come down into the valleys. The roses in the garden of the Queen of Arabia are not so white as thy body. Neither the roses of the garden of the Queen of Arabia, the garden of spices of the Queen of Arabia, nor the feet of the dawn when they light on the leaves, nor the breast of the moon when she lies on the breast of the sea. . . . There is nothing in the world so white as thy body. Suffer me to touch thy body.

IOKANAAN:

Back! daughter of Babylon! By woman came evil into the world. Speak not to me. I will not listen to thee. I listen but to the voice of the Lord God.

SALOME:

Thy body is hideous. It is like the body of a leper. It is like a plastered wall, where vipers have crawled; like a plastered wall where the scorpions have made their nest. It is like a whited sepulchre, full of loathsome things. It is horrible, thy body is horrible. It is of thy hair that I am enamoured, Iokanaan. Thy hair is like clusters of grapes, like the clusters of black grapes that hang from the vine-trees of Edom in the land of the Edomites. Thy hair is like the cedars of Lebanon, like the great cedars of Lebanon that give their shade to the lions and to the robbers who would hide in them by day. The long black nights, when the moon hides her face, when the stars are afraid, are not so black as thy hair. The silence that dwells in the forest is not so black. There is nothing in the world that is so black as thy hair. . . . Suffer me to touch thy hair.

IOKANAAN:

Back, daughter of Sodom! Touch me not. Profane not the temple of the Lord God.

SALOME:

Thy hair is horrible. It is covered with mire and dust. It is like a crown of thorns placed on thy head. It is like a knot of serpents coiled round thy neck. I love not thy hair. . . . It is thy mouth that I desire, Iokanaan. Thy mouth is like a band of scarlet on a tower of ivory. It is like a pomegranate cut in twain with a knife of ivory. The pomegranate flowers that blossom in the gardens of Tyre, and are redder than roses, are not so red. The red blasts of trumpets that herald the approach of kings, and make afraid the enemy, are not so red. Thy mouth is redder than the feet of those who tread the wine in the wine-press. It is redder than the feet of the doves who inhabit the temples and are fed by the priests. It is redder than the feet of him who cometh from a forest where he hath slain a lion, and seen gilded tigers. Thy mouth is like a branch of coral that fishers have found in the twilight of the sea, the coral that they keep for the kings! . . . It is like the vermilion that the Moabites find in the mines of Moab, the vermilion that the kings take from them. It is like the bow of the King of the Persians, that is painted with vermilion, and is tipped with coral. There is nothing in the world so red as thy mouth. . . . Suffer me to kiss thy mouth.

IOKANAAN:

Never! daughter of Babylon! Daughter of Sodom! never!

SALOME:

I will kiss thy mouth, Iokanaan. I will kiss thy mouth.

THE YOUNG SYRIAN:

Princess, Princess, thou who art like a garden of myrrh, thou who art the dove of all doves, look not at this man, look not at him! Do not speak such words to him. I cannot endure it. . . . Princess, do not speak these things.

SALOME:

I will kiss thy mouth, Iokanaan.

THE YOUNG SYRIAN:

Ah! [*He kills himself, and falls between Salome and Iokanaan.*]

THE PAGE OF HERODIAS:

The young Syrian has slain himself! The young captain has slain himself! He has slain himself who was my friend! I gave him a little box of perfumes and ear-rings wrought in silver, and now he has killed himself! Ah, did he not say that some misfortune would happen? I, too, said it, and it has come to pass. Well I knew that the moon was seeking a dead thing, but I knew not that it was he whom she sought. Ah! why did I not hide him from the moon? If I had hidden him in a cavern she would not have seen him.

FIRST SOLDIER:

Princess, the young captain has just slain himself.

SALOME:

Suffer me to kiss thy mouth, Iokanaan.

IOKANAAN:

Art thou not afraid, daughter of Herodias? Did I not tell thee that I had heard in the palace the beating of the wings of the angel of death, and hath he not come, the angel of death?

SALOME:

Suffer me to kiss thy mouth.

IOKANAAN:

Daughter of adultery, there is but one who can save thee. It is He of whom I spake. Go seek Him. He is in a boat on the sea of Galilee, and He talketh with His disciples. Kneel down on the shore of the sea, and call unto Him by His name. When He cometh to thee, and to all who call on Him He cometh, bow thyself at His feet and ask of Him the remission of thy sins.

SALOME:
Suffer me to kiss thy mouth.

IOKANAAN:
Cursed be thou! daughter of an incestuous mother, be thou accursed!

SALOME:
I will kiss thy mouth, Iokanaan.

IOKANAAN:
I will not look at thee. Thou art accursed, Salome, thou art accursed. [*He goes down into the cistern.*]

SALOME:
I will kiss thy mouth, Iokanaan; I will kiss thy mouth.

FIRST SOLDIER:
We must bear away the body to another place. The Tetrarch does not care to see dead bodies, save the bodies of those whom he himself has slain.

THE PAGE OF HERODIAS:
He was my brother, and nearer to me than a brother. I gave him a little box full of perfumes, and a ring of agate that he wore always on his hand. In the evening we were wont to walk by the river, and among the almond-trees, and he used to tell me of the things of his country. He spake ever very low. The sound of his voice was like the sound of the flute, of one who playeth upon the flute. Also he had much joy to gaze at himself in the river. I used to reproach him for that.

SECOND SOLDIER:
You are right; we must hide the body. The Tetrarch must not see it.

FIRST SOLDIER:
The Tetrarch will not come to this place. He never comes on the terrace. He is too much afraid of the prophet. [*Enter Herod, Herodias, and all the Court.*]

HEROD:

Where is Salome? Where is the Princess? Why did she not return to the banquet as I commanded her? Ah! there she is!

HERODIAS:

You must not look at her! You are always looking at her!

HEROD:

The moon has a strange look tonight. Has she not a strange look? She is like a mad woman, a mad woman who is seeking everywhere for lovers. She is naked too. She is quite naked. The clouds are seeking to clothe her nakedness, but she will not let them. She shows herself naked in the sky. She reels through the clouds like a drunken woman. . . . I am sure she is looking for lovers. Does she not reel like a drunken woman? She is like a mad woman, is she not?

HERODIAS:

No; the moon is like the moon, that is all. Let us go within . . . We have nothing to do here.

HEROD:

I will stay here! Manasseh, lay carpets there. Light torches. Bring forth the ivory tables, and the tables of jasper. The air here is sweet. I will drink more wine with my guests. We must show all honours to the ambassadors of Cæsar.

HERODIAS:

It is not because of them that you remain.

HEROD:

Yes; the air is very sweet. Come, Herodias, our guests await us. Ah! I have slipped! I have slipped in blood! It is an ill omen. It is a very ill omen. Wherefore is there blood here? . . . and this body, what does this body here? Think you I am like the King of Egypt, who gives no feast to his guests but that he shows them a corpse? Whose is it? I will not look on it.

FIRST SOLDIER:

It is our captain, sire. It is the young Syrian whom you made captain of the guard but three days gone.

HEROD:

I issued no order that he should be slain.

SECOND SOLDIER:

He slew himself, sire.

HEROD:

For what reason? I had made him captain of my guard!

SECOND SOLDIER:

We do not know, sire. But with his own hand he slew himself.

HEROD:

That seems strange to me. I had thought it was but the Roman philosophers who slew themselves. Is it not true, Tigellinus, that the philosophers at Rome slay themselves?

TIGELLINUS:

There be some who slay themselves, sire. They are the Stoics. The Stoics are people of no cultivation. They are ridiculous people. I myself regard them as being perfectly ridiculous.

HEROD:

I also. It is ridiculous to kill one's self.

TIGELLINUS:

Everybody at Rome laughs at them. The Emperor has written a satire against them. It is recited everywhere.

HEROD:

Ah! he has written a satire against them? Cæsar is wonderful. He can do everything. . . . It is strange that the young Syrian has slain himself. I am sorry he has slain himself. I am very sorry. For he was fair to look upon. He was even very fair. He had very languorous eyes. I remember that I saw that he looked languorously at Salome. Truly, I thought he looked too much at her.

HERODIAS:

There are others who look too much at her.

HEROD:

His father was a king. I drave him from his kingdom. And of

his mother, who was a queen, you made a slave, Herodias. So he was here as my guest, as it were, and for that reason I made him my captain. I am sorry he is dead. Ho! why have you left the body here? It must be taken to some other place. I will not look at it,— away with it! [*They take away the body.*] It is cold here. There is a wind blowing. Is there not a wind blowing?

HERODIAS:

No; there is no wind.

HEROD:

I tell you there is a wind that blows. . . . And I hear in the air something that is like the beating of wings, like the beating of vast wings. Do you not hear it?

HERODIAS:

I hear nothing.

HEROD:

I hear it no longer. But I heard it. It was the blowing of the wind. It has passed away. But no, I hear it again. Do you not hear it? It is just like a beating of wings.

HERODIAS:

I tell you there is nothing. You are ill. Let us go within.

HEROD:

I am not ill. It is your daughter who is sick to death. Never have I seen her so pale.

HERODIAS:

I have told you not to look at her.

HEROD:

Pour me forth wine. [*Wine is brought.*] Salome, come drink a little wine with me. I have here a wine that is exquisite. Caesar himself sent it me. Dip into it thy little red lips, that I may drain the cup.

SALOME:

I am not thirsty, Tetrarch.

HEROD:

You hear how she answers me, this daughter of yours?

HERODIAS:

She does right. Why are you always gazing at her?

HEROD:

Bring me ripe fruits. [*Fruits are brought.*] Salome, come and eat fruits with me. I love to see in a fruit the mark of thy little teeth. Bite but a little of this fruit, that I may eat what is left.

SALOME:

I am not hungry, Tetrarch.

HEROD:

[*To Herodias.*] You see how you have brought up this daughter of yours.

HERODIAS:

My daughter and I come of a royal race. As for thee, thy father was a camel driver! He was a thief and a robber to boot!

HEROD:

Thou liest!

HERODIAS:

Thou knowest well that it is true.

HEROD:

Salome, come and sit next to me. I will give thee the throne of thy mother.

SALOME:

I am not tired, Tetrarch.

HERODIAS:

You see in what regard she holds you.

HEROD:

Bring me—— What is it that I desire? I forget. Ah! ah! I remember.

THE VOICE OF IOKANAAN:

Behold the time is come! That which I foretold has come to pass. The day that I spake of is at hand.

HERODIAS:

Bid him be silent. I will not listen to his voice. This man is for ever hurling insults against me.

HEROD:

He has said nothing against you. Besides, he is a very great prophet.

HERODIAS:

I do not believe in prophets. Can a man tell what will come to pass? No man knows it. Also he is forever insulting me. But I think you are afraid of him. . . . I know well that you are afraid of him.

HEROD:

I am not afraid of him. I am afraid of no man.

HERODIAS:

I tell you you are afraid of him. If you are not afraid of him why do you not deliver him to the Jews who for these six months past have been clamouring for him?

A JEW:

Truly, my lord, it were better to deliver him into our hands.

HEROD:

Enough on this subject. I have already given you my answer. I will not deliver him into your hands. He is a holy man. He is a man who has seen God.

A JEW:

That cannot be. There is no man who hath seen God since the prophet Elias. He is the last man who saw God face to face. In these days God doth not show Himself. God hideth Himself. Therefore great evils have come upon the land.

ANOTHER JEW:

Verily, no man knoweth if Elias the prophet did indeed see God. Peradventure it was but the shadow of God that he saw.

A THIRD JEW:

God is at no time hidden. He showeth Himself at all times and in all places. God is in what is evil even as He is in what is good.

A FOURTH JEW:

Thou shouldst not say that. It is a very dangerous doctrine. It is a doctrine that cometh from Alexandria, where men teach the philosophy of the Greeks. And the Greeks are Gentiles. They are not even circumcised.

A FIFTH JEW:

No man can tell how God worketh. His ways are very dark. It may be that the things which we call evil are good, and the things which we call good are evil. There is no knowledge of anything. We can but bow our heads to His will, for God is very strong. He breaketh in pieces the strong together with the weak, for He regardeth not any man.

FIRST JEW:

Thou speakest truly. Verily, God is terrible. He breaketh in pieces the strong and the weak as men break corn in a mortar. But as for this man, he hath never seen God. No man hath seen God since the prophet Elias.

HERODIAS:

Make them be silent. They weary me.

HEROD:

But I have heard it said that Iokanaan is in very truth your prophet Elias.

THE JEW:

That cannot be. It is more than three hundred years since the days of the prophet Elias.

HEROD:

There be some who say that this man is Elias the prophet.

A NAZARENE:

I am sure that he is Elias the prophet.

THE JEW:

Nay, but he is not Elias the prophet.

THE VOICE OF IOKANAAN:

Behold the day is at hand, the day of the Lord, and I hear upon the mountains the feet of Him who shall be the Saviour of the world.

HEROD:

What does that mean? The Saviour of the world?

TIGELLINUS:

It is a title that Cæsar adopts.

HEROD:

But Cæsar is not coming into Judæa. Only yesterday I received letters from Rome. They contained nothing concerning this matter. And you, Tigellinus, who were at Rome during the winter, you heard nothing concerning this matter, did you?

TIGELLINUS:

Sire, I heard nothing concerning the matter. I was but explaining the title. It is one of Cæsar's titles.

HEROD:

But Cæsar cannot come. He is too gouty. They say that his feet are like the feet of an elephant. Also there are reasons of state. He who leaves Rome loses Rome. He will not come. Howbeit, Cæsar is lord, he will come if such be his pleasure. Nevertheless, I think he will not come.

FIRST NAZARENE:

It was not concerning Cæsar that the prophet spake these words, sire.

HEROD:

How?—it was not concerning Cæsar?

FIRST NAZARENE:

No, my lord.

HEROD:

Concerning whom then did he speak?

FIRST NAZARENE:

Concerning Messias, who hath come.

A JEW:

Messias hath not come.

FIRST NAZARENE:

He hath come, and everywhere He worketh miracles!

HERODIAS:

Ho! ho! miracles! I do not believe in miracles. I have seen too many. [*To the Page.*] My fan.

FIRST NAZARENE:

This Man worketh true miracles. Thus, at a marriage which took place in a little town of Galilee, a town of some importance, He changed water into wine. Certain persons who were present related it to me. Also He healed two lepers that were seated before the Gate of Capernaum simply by touching them.

SECOND NAZARENE:

Nay; it was two blind men that He healed at Capernaum.

FIRST NAZARENE:

Nay; they were lepers. But He hath healed blind people also, and He was seen on a mountain talking with angels.

A SADDUCEE:

Angels do not exist.

A PHARISEE:

Angels exist, but I do not believe that this Man has talked with them.

FIRST NAZARENE:

He was seen by a great multitude of people talking with angels.

HERODIAS:

How these men weary me! They are ridiculous! They are altogether ridiculous! [*To the Page.*] Well! my fan? [*The Page gives her the fan.*] You have a dreamer's look. You must not dream. It is only sick people who dream. [*She strikes the Page with her fan.*]

SECOND NAZARENE:

There is also the miracle of the daughter of Jairus.

FIRST NAZARENE:

Yea, that is sure. No man can gainsay it.

HERODIAS:

Those men are mad. They have looked too long on the moon. Command them to be silent.

HEROD:
   What is this miracle of the daughter of Jairus?

FIRST NAZARENE:
   The daughter of Jairus was dead. This Man raised her from the dead.

HEROD:
   How! He raises people from the dead?

FIRST NAZARENE:
   Yea, sire; He raiseth the dead.

HEROD:
   I do not wish Him to do that. I forbid Him to do that. I suffer no man to raise the dead. This Man must be found and told that I forbid him to raise the dead. Where is this Man at present?

SECOND NAZARENE:
   He is in every place, my lord, but it is hard to find Him.

FIRST NAZARENE:
   It is said that He is now in Samaria.

A JEW:
   It is easy to see that this is not Messias, if He is in Samaria. It is not to the Samaritans that Messias shall come. The Samaritans are accursed. They bring no offerings to the Temple.

SECOND NAZARENE:
   He left Samaria a few days since. I think that at the present moment He is in the neighbourhood of Jerusalem.

FIRST NAZARENE:
   No; He is not there. I have just come from Jerusalem. For two months they have had no tidings of Him.

HEROD:
   No matter! But let them find Him, and tell Him, thus saith Herod the King, "I will not suffer Thee to raise the dead." To change water into wine, to heal the lepers and the blind. . . . He may do these things if He will. I say nothing against these things. In truth I hold it a kindly deed to heal a leper. But no man shall raise the dead. . . . It would be terrible if the dead came back.

THE VOICE OF IOKANAAN:

Ah! the wanton one! the harlot! Ah! the daughter of Babylon with her golden eyes and her gilded eyelids! Thus saith the Lord God, Let there come up against her a multitude of men. Let the people take stones and stone her. . . .

HERODIAS:

Command him to be silent!

THE VOICE OF IOKANAAN:

Let the captains of the hosts pierce her with their swords, let them crush her beneath their shields.

HERODIAS:

Nay, but it is infamous.

THE VOICE OF IOKANAAN:

It is thus that I will wipe out all wickedness from the earth, and that all women shall learn not to imitate her abominations.

HERODIAS:

You hear what he says against me? You suffer him to revile her who is your wife!

HEROD:

He did not speak your name.

HERODIAS:

What does that matter? You know well that it is I whom he seeks to revile. And I am your wife, am I not?

HEROD:

Of a truth, dear and noble Herodias, you are my wife, and before that you were the wife of my brother.

HERODIAS:

It was thou didst snatch me from his arms.

HEROD:

Of a truth I was stronger than he was. . . . But let us not talk of that matter. I do not desire to talk of it. It is the cause of the terrible words the prophet has spoken. Peradventure on account of it a misfortune will come. Let us not speak of this matter. Noble Herodias, we are not mindful of our guests. Fill thou my cup, my well-beloved. Ho! fill with wine the great goblets of silver, and the great goblets of glass. I will drink to Cæsar. There are Romans here, we must drink to Cæsar.

ALL:

Cæsar! Cæsar!

HEROD:

Do you not see your daughter, how pale she is?

HERODIAS:

What is it to you if she be pale or not?

HEROD:

Never have I seen her so pale.

HERODIAS:

You must not look at her.

THE VOICE OF IOKANAAN:

In that day the sun shall become black like sackcloth of hair, and the moon shall become like blood, and the stars of the heaven shall fall upon the earth like unripe figs that fall from the fig-tree, and the kings of the earth shall be afraid.

HERODIAS:

Ah! ah! I should like to see that day of which he speaks, when the moon shall become like blood, and when the stars shall fall upon the earth like unripe figs. This prophet talks like a drunken man, . . . but I cannot suffer the sound of his voice. I hate his voice. Command him to be silent.

HEROD:

I will not. I cannot understand what it is that he saith, but it may be an omen.

HERODIAS:

I do not believe in omens. He speaks like a drunken man.

HEROD:

It may be he is drunk with the wine of God.

HERODIAS:

What wine is that, the wine of God? From what vineyards is it gathered? In what winepress may one find it?

HEROD:

[*From this point he looks all the while at Salome.*] Tigellinus, when you were at Rome of late, did the Emperor speak with you on the subject of . . . ?

TIGELLINUS:

On what subject, my lord?

HEROD:

On what subject? Ah! I asked you a question, did I not? I have forgotten what I would have asked you.

HERODIAS:

You are looking again at my daughter. You must not look at her. I have already said so.

HEROD:

You say nothing else.

HERODIAS:

I say it again.

HEROD:

And that restoration of the Temple about which they have talked so much, will anything be done? They say that the veil of the Sanctuary has disappeared, do they not?

HERODIAS:

It was thyself didst steal it. Thou speakest at random and without wit. I will not stay here. Let us go within.

HEROD:

Dance for me, Salome.

HERODIAS:

I will not have her dance.

SALOME:
  I have no desire to dance, Tetrarch.

HEROD:
  Salome, daughter of Herodias, dance for me.

HERODIAS:
  Peace. Let her alone.

HEROD:
  I command thee to dance, Salome.

SALOME:
  I will not dance, Tetrarch.

HERODIAS:
  [*Laughing.*] You see how she obeys you.

HEROD:
  What is it to me whether she dance or not? It is nought to me. Tonight I am happy. I am exceeding happy. Never have I been so happy.

FIRST SOLDIER:
  The Tetrarch has a sombre look. Has he not a sombre look?

SECOND SOLDIER:
  Yes, he has a sombre look.

HEROD:
  Wherefore should I not be happy? Cæsar, who is lord of the world, Cæsar, who is lord of all things, loves me well. He has just sent me most precious gifts. Also he has promised me to summon to Rome the King of Cappadocia, who is mine enemy. It may be that at Rome he will crucify him, for he is able to do all things that he has a mind to do. Verily, Cæsar is lord. Therefore I do well to be happy. I am very happy, never have I been so happy. There is nothing in the world that can mar my happiness.

THE VOICE OF IOKANAAN:
  He shall be seated on his throne. He shall be clothed in scarlet and purple. In his hand he shall bear a golden cup full of his blasphemies. And the angel of the Lord shall smite him. He shall be eaten of worms.

HERODIAS:

You hear what he says about you. He says that you shall be eaten of worms.

HEROD:

It is not of me that he speaks. He speaks never against me. It is of the King of Cappadocia that he speaks; the King of Cappadocia who is mine enemy. It is he who shall be eaten of worms. It is not I. Never has he spoken word against me, this prophet, save that I sinned in taking to wife the wife of my brother. It may be he is right. For, of a truth, you are sterile.

HERODIAS:

I am sterile, I? You say that, you that are ever looking at my daughter, you that would have her dance for your pleasure? You speak as a fool. I have borne a child. You have gotten no child, no, not on one of your slaves. It is you who are sterile, not I.

HEROD:

Peace, woman! I say that you are sterile. You have borne me no child, and the prophet says that our marriage is not a true marriage. He says that it is a marriage of incest, a marriage that will bring evils. . . . I fear he is right; I am sure that he is right. But it is not the hour to speak of these things. I would be happy at this moment. Of a truth, I am happy. There is nothing I lack.

HERODIAS:

I am glad you are of so fair a humour tonight. It is not your custom. But it is late. Let us go within. Do not forget that we hunt at sunrise. All honours must be shown to Cæsar's ambassadors, must they not?

SECOND SOLDIER:

The Tetrarch has a sombre look.

FIRST SOLDIER:

Yes, he has a sombre look.

HEROD:

Salome, Salome, dance for me. I pray thee dance for me. I am sad tonight. Yes, I am passing sad tonight. When I came hither I slipped in blood, which is an ill omen; also I heard in the air a beating of wings, a beating of giant wings. I cannot tell what that may mean. . . . I am sad tonight. Therefore dance for me. Dance for me, Salome, I beseech thee. If thou dancest for me thou mayest ask of me what thou wilt, and I will give it thee. Yes, dance for me, Salome, and whatsoever thou shalt ask of me I will give it thee, even unto the half of my kingdom.

SALOME:

[*Rising.*] Will you indeed give me whatsoever I shall ask of you, Tetrarch?

HERODIAS:

Do not dance, my daughter.

HEROD:

Whatsoever thou shalt ask of me, even unto the half of my kingdom.

SALOME:

You swear it, Tetrarch?

HEROD:

I swear it, Salome.

HERODIAS:

Do not dance, my daughter.

SALOME:

By what will you swear this thing, Tetrarch?

HEROD:

By my life, by my crown, by my gods. Whatsoever thou shalt desire I will give it thee, even to the half of my kingdom, if thou wilt but dance for me. O Salome, Salome, dance for me!

SALOME:

You have sworn an oath, Tetrarch.

HEROD:

I have sworn an oath.

HERODIAS:

My daughter, do not dance.

HEROD:

Even to the half of my kingdom. Thou wilt be passing fair as a queen, Salome, if it please thee to ask for the half of my kingdom. Will she not be fair as a queen? Ah! it is cold here! There is an icy wind, and I hear . . . wherefore do I hear in the air this beating of wings? Ah! one might fancy a huge black bird that hovers over the terrace. Why can I not see it, this bird? The beat of its wings is terrible. The breath of the wind of its wings is terrible. It is a chill wind. Nay, but it is not cold, it is hot. I am choking. Pour water on my hands. Give me snow to eat. Loosen my mantle. Quick! quick! loosen my mantle. Nay, but leave it. It is my garland that hurts me, my garland of roses. The flowers are like fire. They have burned my forehead. [*He tears the wreath from his head, and throws it on the table.*] Ah! I can breathe now. How red those petals are! They are like stains of blood on the cloth. That does not matter. It is not wise to find symbols in everything that one sees. It makes life too full of terrors. It were better to say that stains of blood are as lovely as rose-petals. It were better far to say that. . . . But we will not speak of this. Now I am happy. I am passing happy. Have I not the right to be happy? Your daughter is going to dance for me. Wilt thou not dance for me, Salome? Thou hast promised to dance for me.

HERODIAS:

I will not have her dance.

SALOME:

I will dance for you, Tetrarch.

HEROD:

You hear what your daughter says. She is going to dance for me. Thou doest well to dance for me, Salome. And when thou hast danced for me, forget not to ask of me whatsoever thou hast a mind to ask. Whatsoever thou shalt desire I will give it thee, even to the half of my kingdom. I have sworn it, have I not?

SALOME:

Thou hast sworn it, Tetrarch.

HEROD:

And I have never failed of my word. I am not of those who

break their oaths. I know not how to lie. I am the slave of my word, and my word is the word of a king. The King of Cappadocia had ever a lying tongue, but he is no true king. He is a coward. Also he owes me money that he will not repay. He has even insulted my ambassadors. He has spoken words that were wounding. But Cæsar will crucify him when he comes to Rome. I know that Cæsar will crucify him. And if he crucify him not, yet will he die, being eaten of worms. The prophet has prophesied it. Well! Wherefore dost thou tarry, Salome?

SALOME:

I am waiting until my slaves bring perfumes to me and the seven veils, and take from off my feet my sandals. [*Slaves bring perfumes and the seven veils, and take off the sandals of Salome.*]

HEROD:

Ah, thou art to dance with naked feet! 'Tis well! 'tis well! Thy little feet will be like white doves. They will be like little white flowers that dance upon the trees. . . . No, no, she is going to dance on blood! There is blood spilt on the ground. She must not dance on blood. It were an evil omen.

HERODIAS:

What is it to thee if she dance on blood? Thou hast waded deep enough in it. . . .

HEROD:

What is it to me? Ah! look at the moon! She has become red. She has become red as blood. Ah! the prophet prophesied truly. He prophesied that the moon would become as blood. Did he not prophesy it? All of ye heard him prophesying it. And now the moon has become as blood. Do ye not see it?

HERODIAS:

Oh yes, I see it well, and the stars are falling like unripe figs, are they not? and the sun is becoming black like sackcloth of hair, and the kings of the earth are afraid. That at least one can see. The prophet is justified of his words in that at least, for truly the kings of the earth are afraid. . . . Let us go within. You are sick. They will say at Rome that you are mad. Let us go within, I tell you.

THE VOICE OF IOKANAAN:

Who is this who cometh from Edom, who is this who cometh from Bozra, whose raiment is dyed with purple, who shineth in the beauty of his garments, who walketh mighty in his greatness? Wherefore is thy raiment stained with scarlet?

HERODIAS:

Let us go within. The voice of that man maddens me. I will not have my daughter dance while he is continually crying out. I will not have her dance while you look at her in this fashion. In a word, I will not have her dance.

HEROD:

Do not rise, my wife, my queen, it will avail thee nothing. I will not go within till she hath danced. Dance, Salome, dance for me.

HERODIAS:

Do not dance, my daughter.

SALOME:

I am ready, Tetrarch. [*Salome dances the dance of the seven veils.*]

HEROD:

Ah! wonderful! wonderful! You see that she has danced for me, your daughter. Come near, Salome, come near, that I may give thee thy fee. Ah! I pay a royal price to those who dance for my pleasure. I will pay thee royally. I will give thee whatsoever thy soul desireth. What wouldst thou have? Speak.

SALOME:

[*Kneeling.*] I would that they presently bring me in a silver charger . . .

HEROD:

[*Laughing.*] In a silver charger? Surely yes, in a silver charger. She is charming, is she not? What is it that thou wouldst have in a silver charger, O sweet and fair Salome, thou that art fairer than all the daughters of Judaea? What wouldst thou have them bring thee in a silver charger? Tell me. Whatsoever it may be, thou shalt receive it. My treasures belong to thee. What is it that thou wouldst have, Salome?

SALOME:

[*Rising.*] The head of Iokanaan.

HERODIAS:

Ah! that is well said, my daughter.

HEROD:

No, no!

HERODIAS:

That is well said, my daughter.

HEROD:

No, no, Salome. It is not that thou desirest. Do not listen to thy mother's voice. She is ever giving thee evil counsel. Do not heed her.

SALOME:

It is not my mother's voice that I heed. It is for mine own pleasure that I ask the head of Iokanaan in a silver charger. You have sworn an oath, Herod. Forget not that you have sworn an oath.

HEROD:

I know it. I have sworn an oath by my gods. I know it well. But I pray thee, Salome, ask of me something else. Ask of me the half of my kingdom, and I will give it thee. But ask not of me what thy lips have asked.

SALOME:

I ask of you the head of Iokanaan.

HEROD:

No, no, I will not give it thee.

SALOME:

You have sworn an oath, Herod.

HERODIAS:

Yes, you have sworn an oath. Everybody heard you. You swore it before everybody.

HEROD:

Peace, woman! It is not to you I speak.

HERODIAS:

My daughter has done well to ask the head of Iokanaan. He has covered me with insults. He has said unspeakable things against me. One can see that she loves her mother well. Do not yield, my daughter. He has sworn an oath, he has sworn an oath.

HEROD:

Peace! Speak not to me! . . . Salome, I pray thee be not stubborn. I have ever been kind toward thee. I have ever loved thee. . . . It may be that I have loved thee too much. Therefore ask not this thing of me. This is a terrible thing, an awful thing to ask of me. Surely, I think thou art jesting. The head of a man that is cut from his body is ill to look upon, is it not? It is not meet that the eyes of a virgin should look upon such a thing. What pleasure couldst thou have in it? There is no pleasure that thou couldst have in it. No, no, it is not that thou desirest. Hearken to me. I have an emerald, a great emerald and round, that the minion of Cæsar has sent unto me. When thou lookest through this emerald thou canst see that which passeth afar off. Cæsar himself carries such an emerald when he goes to the circus. But my emerald is the larger. I know well that it is the larger. It is the largest emerald in the whole world. Thou wilt take that, wilt thou not? Ask it of me and I will give it thee.

SALOME:

I demand the head of Iokanaan.

HEROD:

Thou art not listening. Thou art not listening. Suffer me to speak, Salome.

SALOME:

The head of Iokanaan!

HEROD:

No, no, thou wouldst not have that. Thou sayest that but to trouble me, because that I have looked at thee and ceased not this night. It is true, I have looked at thee and ceased not this night. Thy beauty has troubled me. Thy beauty has grievously troubled me, and I have looked at thee overmuch. Nay, but I will look at thee no more. One should not look at anything. Neither at things, nor at people should one look. Only in mirrors is it well to look, for mirrors do but show us masks. Oh! oh! bring wine! I thirst. . . . Salome, Salome, let us be as friends. Bethink thee. . . . Ah! what would I say? What was 't? Ah! I remember it! . . . Salome,—nay but come nearer to me; I fear thou wilt not hear my words,—Salome, thou knowest my white peacocks, my beautiful white peacocks, that walk in the garden between the myrtles and the tall cypress-trees. Their beaks are gilded with gold and the grains that they eat are smeared with gold, and their feet are stained with purple. When they cry out the rain comes, and the moon shows herself in the heavens when they spread their tails. Two by two they walk between the cypress-trees and the black myrtles, and each has a slave to tend it. Sometimes they fly across the trees, and anon they couch in the grass, and round the pools of the water. There are not in all the world birds so wonderful. I know that Cæsar himself has no birds so fair as my birds. I will give thee fifty of my peacocks. They will follow thee whithersoever thou goest, and in the midst of them thou wilt be like unto the moon in the midst of a great white cloud. . . . I will give them to thee, all. I have but a hundred, and in the whole world there is no king who has peacocks like unto my peacocks. But I will give them all to thee. Only thou must loose me from my oath, and must not ask of me that which thy lips have asked of me. [*He empties the cup of wine.*]

SALOME:
    Give me the head of Iokanaan!

HERODIAS:
    Well said, my daughter! As for you, you are ridiculous with your peacocks.

HEROD:
    Peace! you are always crying out. You cry out like a beast of prey. You must not cry in such fashion. Your voice wearies me. Peace, I tell you! . . . Salome, think on what thou art doing. It may be that this man comes from God. He is a holy man. The finger of God has touched him. God has put terrible words into his mouth. In the palace, as in the desert, God is ever with him. . . . It may be that He is, at least. One cannot tell, but it is possi-

ble that God is with him and for him. If he die also, peradventure some evil may befall me. Verily, he has said that evil will befall some one on the day whereon he dies. On whom should it fall if it fall not on me? Remember, I slipped in blood when I came hither. Also did I not hear a beating of wings in the air, a beating of vast wings? These are ill omens. And there were other things. I am sure that there were other things, though I saw them not. Thou wouldst not that some evil should befall me, Salome? Listen to me again.

SALOME:

Give me the head of Iokanaan!

HEROD:

Ah! thou art not listening to me. Be calm. As for me, am I not calm? I am altogether calm. Listen. I have jewels hidden in this place—jewels that thy mother even has never seen; jewels that are marvellous to look at. I have a collar of pearls, set in four rows. They are like unto moons chained with rays of silver. They are even as half a hundred moons caught in a golden net. On the ivory breast of a queen they have rested. Thou shalt be as fair as a queen when thou wearest them. I have amethysts of two kinds; one that is black like wine, and one that is red like wine that one has coloured with water. I have topazes yellow as are the eyes of tigers, and topazes that are pink as the eyes of a wood-pigeon, and green topazes that are as the eyes of cats. I have opals that burn always, with a flame that is cold as ice, opals that make sad men's minds, and are afraid of the shadows. I have onyxes like the eyeballs of a dead woman. I have moonstones that change when the moon changes, and are wan when they see the sun. I have sapphires big like eggs, and as blue as blue flowers. The sea wanders within them, and the moon comes never to trouble the blue of their waves. I have chrysolites and beryls, and chrysoprases and rubies; I have sardonyx and hyacinth stones, and stones of chalcedony, and I will give them all unto thee, all, and other things will I add to them. The King of the Indies has but even now sent me four fans fashioned from the feathers of parrots, and the King of Numidia a garment of ostrich feathers. I have a crystal, into which it is not lawful for a woman to look, nor may young men behold it until they have been beaten with rods. In a coffer of nacre I have three wondrous turquoises. He who wears them on his forehead can imagine things which are not, and he who carries them in his hand can turn the fruitful woman into a woman that is barren. These are great treasures. They are treasures above all price. But this is not all. In an ebony coffer I have two cups of amber that are like apples of pure gold. If an enemy pour poison into these cups they become like apples of silver. In a coffer incrusted with amber I have sandals incrusted with glass. I have mantles that have been brought from the land of the Seres, and bracelets decked about with carbuncles and with jade that come from the city of Euphrates. . . . What desirest thou more than this, Salome? Tell me the thing that thou desirest, and I will give it thee. All that thou askest I will give thee, save one thing only. I will give thee all that is mine, save only the life of one man. I will give thee the mantle of the high priest. I will give thee the veil of the sanctuary.

THE JEWS:
Oh! oh!

SALOME:
Give me the head of Iokanaan!

HEROD:
[*Sinking back in his seat.*] Let her be given what she asks! Of a truth she is her mother's child! [*The first Soldier approaches. Herodias draws from the hand of the Tetrarch the ring of death, and gives it to the Soldier, who straightway bears it to the Executioner. The Executioner looks scared.*] Who has taken my ring? There was a ring on my right hand. Who has drunk my wine? There was wine in my cup. It was full of wine. Some one has drunk it! Oh! surely some evil will befall some one. [*The Executioner goes down into the cistern.*] Ah! wherefore did I give my oath? Hereafter let no king swear an oath. If he keep it not, it is terrible, and if he keep it, it is terrible also.

HERODIAS:
My daughter has done well.

HEROD:
I am sure that some misfortune will happen.

SALOME:

[*She leans over the cistern and listens.*] There is no sound. I hear nothing. Why does he not cry out, this man? Ah! if any man sought to kill me, I would cry out, I would struggle, I would not suffer. . . . Strike, strike, Naaman, strike, I tell you. . . . No, I hear nothing. There is a silence, a terrible silence. Ah! something has fallen upon the ground. I heard something fall. It was the sword of the executioner. He is afraid, this slave. He has dropped his sword. He dares not kill him. He is a coward, this slave! Let soldiers be sent. [*She sees the Page of Herodias and addresses him.*] Come hither. Thou wert the friend of him who is dead, wert thou not? Well, I tell thee, there are not dead men enough. Go to the soldiers and bid them go down and bring me the thing I ask, the thing the Tetrarch has promised me, the thing that is mine. [*The Page recoils. She turns to the soldiers.*] Hither, ye soldiers. Get ye down into this cistern and bring me the head of this man. Tetrarch, Tetrarch, command your soldiers that they bring me the head of Iokanaan.

[A *huge black arm, the arm of the Executioner, comes forth from the cistern, bearing on a silver shield the head of Iokanaan. Salome seizes it. Herod hides his face with his cloak. Herodias smiles and fans herself. The Nazarenes fall on their knees and begin to pray.*]

Ah! thou wouldst not suffer me to kiss thy mouth, Iokanaan. Well! I will kiss it now. I will bite it with my teeth as one bites a ripe fruit. Yes, I will kiss thy mouth, Iokanaan. I said it; did I not say it? I said it. Ah! I will kiss it now. . . . But wherefore dost thou not look at me, Iokanaan? Thine eyes that were so terrible, so full of rage and scorn, are shut now. Wherefore are they shut? Open thine eyes! Lift up thine eyelids, Iokanaan! Wherefore dost thou not look at me? Art thou afraid of me, Iokanaan, that thou wilt not look at me? . . . And thy tongue, that was like a red snake darting poison, it moves no more, it speaks no words, Iokanaan, that scarlet viper that spat its venom upon me. It is strange, is it not? How is it that the red viper stirs no longer? . . . Thou wouldst have none of me, Iokanaan. Thou rejectedst me. Thou didst speak evil words against me. Thou didst bear thyself toward me as to a harlot, as to a woman that is a wanton, to me, Salome, daughter of Herodias, Princess of Judaea! Well, I still live, but thou art dead, and thy head belongs to me. I can do with it what I will. I can throw it to the dogs and to the birds of the air. That which the dogs leave, the birds of the air shall devour. . . . Ah, Iokanaan, Iokanaan, thou wert the man that I loved alone among men! All other men were hateful to me. But thou wert beautiful! Thy body was a column of ivory set upon feet of silver. It was a garden full of doves and lilies of silver. It was a tower of silver decked with shields of ivory. There was nothing in the world so white as thy body. There was nothing in the world so black as thy hair. In the whole world there was nothing so red as thy mouth. Thy voice was a censer that scattered strange perfumes, and when I looked on thee I heard a strange music. Ah! wherefore didst thou not look at me, Iokanaan? With the cloak of thine hands, and with the cloak of thy blasphemies thou didst hide thy face. Thou didst put upon thine eyes the covering of him who would see his God. Well, thou hast seen thy God, Iokanaan, but me, me, thou didst never see. If thou hadst seen me thou hadst loved me. I saw thee, and I loved thee. Oh, how I loved thee! I love thee yet, Iokanaan. I love only thee. . . . I am athirst for thy beauty; I am hungry for thy body; and neither wine nor apples can appease my desire. What shall I do now, Iokanaan? Neither the floods nor the great waters can quench my passion. I was a princess, and thou didst scorn me. I was a virgin, and thou didst take my virginity from me. I was chaste, and thou didst fill my veins with fire. . . . Ah! ah! wherefore didst thou not look at me? If thou hadst looked at me thou hadst loved me. Well I know that thou wouldst have loved me, and the mystery of Love is greater than the mystery of Death.

HEROD:

She is monstrous, thy daughter; I tell thee she is monstrous. In truth, what she has done is a great crime. I am sure that it is a crime against some unknown God.

HERODIAS:

I am well pleased with my daughter. She has done well. And I would stay here now.

HEROD:

[*Rising.*] Ah! There speaks my brother's wife! Come! I will not stay in this place. Come, I tell thee. Surely some terrible thing will befall. Manasseh, Issachar, Ozias, put out the torches. I will not look at things, I will not suffer things to look at me. Put out the torches! Hide the moon! Hide the stars! Let us hide ourselves in our palace, Herodias. I begin to be afraid. [*The slaves put out the torches. The stars disappear. A great cloud crosses the moon and conceals it completely. The stage becomes quite dark. The Tetrarch begins to climb the staircase.*]

THE VOICE OF SALOME:

Ah! I have kissed thy mouth, Iokanaan, I have kissed thy mouth. There was a bitter taste on thy lips. Was it the taste of blood? . . . Nay; but perchance it was the taste of love. . . . They say that love hath a bitter taste. . . . But what matter? what matter? I have kissed thy mouth, Iokanaan, I have kissed thy mouth. [*A ray of moonlight falls on Salome and illumines her.*]

HEROD:

[*Turning round and seeing Salome.*] Kill that woman! [*The soldiers rush forward and crush beneath their shields Salome, daughter of Herodias, Princess of Judaea*].

CURTAIN

DOVER·THRIFT·EDITIONS

All books complete and unabridged. All 5³⁄₁₆" x 8¹⁄₄," paperbound.

A selection of the more than 200 titles in the series.

POETRY

101 GREAT AMERICAN POEMS, The American Poetry & Literacy Project (ed.). (Available in U.S. only.) 40158-8

ENGLISH ROMANTIC POETRY: An Anthology, Stanley Appelbaum (ed.). 256pp. 29282-7

DOVER BEACH AND OTHER POEMS, Matthew Arnold. 112pp. 28037-3

SELECTED POEMS FROM "FLOWERS OF EVIL," Charles Baudelaire. 64pp. 28450-6

BHAGAVADGITA, Bhagavadgita. 112pp. 27782-8

THE BOOK OF PSALMS, King James Bible. 128pp. 27541-8

IMAGIST POETRY: AN ANTHOLOGY, Bob Blaisdell (ed.). 176pp. (Available in U.S. only.) 40875-2

BLAKE'S SELECTED POEMS, William Blake. 96pp. 28517-0

SONGS OF INNOCENCE AND SONGS OF EXPERIENCE, William Blake. 64pp. 27051-3

THE CLASSIC TRADITION OF HAIKU: An Anthology, Faubion Bowers (ed.). 96pp. 29274-6

BEST POEMS OF THE BRONTË SISTERS (ed. by Candace Ward), Emily, Anne, and Charlotte Brontë. 64pp. 29529-X

SONNETS FROM THE PORTUGUESE AND OTHER POEMS, Elizabeth Barrett Browning. 64pp. 27052-1

MY LAST DUCHESS AND OTHER POEMS, Robert Browning. 128pp. 27783-6

POEMS AND SONGS, Robert Burns. 96pp. 26863-2

SELECTED POEMS, George Gordon, Lord Byron. 112pp. 27784-4

SELECTED CANTERBURY TALES, Geoffrey Chaucer. 144pp. 28241-4

THE RIME OF THE ANCIENT MARINER AND OTHER POEMS, Samuel Taylor Coleridge. 80pp. 27266-4

WAR IS KIND AND OTHER POEMS, Stephen Crane. 64pp. 40424-2

THE CAVALIER POETS: An Anthology, Thomas Crofts (ed.). 80pp. 28766-1

SELECTED POEMS, Emily Dickinson. 64pp. 26466-1

SELECTED POEMS, John Donne. 96pp. 27788-7

SELECTED POEMS, Paul Laurence Dunbar. 80pp. 29980-5

"THE WASTE LAND" AND OTHER POEMS, T. S. Eliot. 64pp. (Available in U.S. only.) 40061-1

THE CONCORD HYMN AND OTHER POEMS, Ralph Waldo Emerson. 64pp. 29059-X

THE RUBÁIYÁT OF OMAR KHAYYÁM: FIRST AND FIFTH EDITIONS, Edward FitzGerald. 64pp. 26467-X

A BOY'S WILL AND NORTH OF BOSTON, Robert Frost. 112pp. (Available in U.S. only.) 26866-7

THE ROAD NOT TAKEN AND OTHER POEMS, Robert Frost. 64pp. (Available in U.S. only.) 27550-7

HARDY'S SELECTED POEMS, Thomas Hardy. 80pp. 28753-X

"GOD'S GRANDEUR" AND OTHER POEMS, Gerard Manley Hopkins. 80pp. 28729-7

A SHROPSHIRE LAD, A. E. Housman. 64pp. 26468-8

LYRIC POEMS, John Keats. 80pp. 26871-3

DOVER·THRIFT·EDITIONS

POETRY

FICTION

FLATLAND: A ROMANCE OF MANY DIMENSIONS, Edwin A. Abbott. 96pp. 27263-X

SHORT STORIES, Louisa May Alcott. 64pp. 29063-8

WINESBURG, OHIO, Sherwood Anderson. 160pp. 28269-4

PERSUASION, Jane Austen. 224pp. 29555-9

PRIDE AND PREJUDICE, Jane Austen. 272pp. 28473-5

SENSE AND SENSIBILITY, Jane Austen. 272pp. 29049-2

LOOKING BACKWARD, Edward Bellamy. 160pp. 29038-7

BEOWULF, Beowulf (trans. by R. K. Gordon). 64pp. 27264-8

CIVIL WAR STORIES, Ambrose Bierce. 128pp. 28038-1

"THE MOONLIT ROAD" AND OTHER GHOST AND HORROR STORIES, Ambrose Bierce (John Grafton, ed.) 96pp. 40056-5

WUTHERING HEIGHTS, Emily Brontë. 256pp. 29256-8

THE THIRTY-NINE STEPS, John Buchan. 96pp. 28201-5

TARZAN OF THE APES, Edgar Rice Burroughs. 224pp. (Available in U.S. only.) 29570-2

ALICE'S ADVENTURES IN WONDERLAND, Lewis Carroll. 96pp. 27543-4

THROUGH THE LOOKING-GLASS, Lewis Carroll. 128pp. 40878-7

MY ÁNTONIA, Willa Cather. 176pp. 28240-6

O PIONEERS!, Willa Cather. 128pp. 27785-2

PAUL'S CASE AND OTHER STORIES, Willa Cather. 64pp. 29057-3

FIVE GREAT SHORT STORIES, Anton Chekhov. 96pp. 26463-7

TALES OF CONJURE AND THE COLOR LINE, Charles Waddell Chesnutt. 128pp. 40426-9

FAVORITE FATHER BROWN STORIES, G. K. Chesterton. 96pp. 27545-0

THE AWAKENING, Kate Chopin. 128pp. 27786-0

A PAIR OF SILK STOCKINGS AND OTHER STORIES, Kate Chopin. 64pp. 29264-9

HEART OF DARKNESS, Joseph Conrad. 80pp. 26464-5

LORD JIM, Joseph Conrad. 256pp. 40650-4

THE SECRET SHARER AND OTHER STORIES, Joseph Conrad. 128pp. 27546-9

THE "LITTLE REGIMENT" AND OTHER CIVIL WAR STORIES, Stephen Crane. 80pp. 29557-5

THE OPEN BOAT AND OTHER STORIES, Stephen Crane. 128pp. 27547-7

THE RED BADGE OF COURAGE, Stephen Crane. 112pp. 26465-3

MOLL FLANDERS, Daniel Defoe. 256pp. 29093-X

ROBINSON CRUSOE, Daniel Defoe. 288pp. 40427-7

A CHRISTMAS CAROL, Charles Dickens. 80pp. 26865-9

THE CRICKET ON THE HEARTH AND OTHER CHRISTMAS STORIES, Charles Dickens. 128pp. 28039-X

A TALE OF TWO CITIES, Charles Dickens. 304pp. 40651-2

THE DOUBLE, Fyodor Dostoyevsky. 128pp. 29572-9

THE GAMBLER, Fyodor Dostoyevsky. 112pp. 29081-6

NOTES FROM THE UNDERGROUND, Fyodor Dostoyevsky. 96pp. 27053-X

THE ADVENTURE OF THE DANCING MEN AND OTHER STORIES, Sir Arthur Conan Doyle. 80pp. 29558-3

THE HOUND OF THE BASKERVILLES, Arthur Conan Doyle. 128pp. 28214-7

THE LOST WORLD, Arthur Conan Doyle. 176pp. 40060-3

DOVER · THRIFT · EDITIONS

FICTION

SIX GREAT SHERLOCK HOLMES STORIES, Sir Arthur Conan Doyle. 112pp. 27055-6

SHORT STORIES, Theodore Dreiser. 112pp. 28215-5

SILAS MARNER, George Eliot. 160pp. 29246-0

THIS SIDE OF PARADISE, F. Scott Fitzgerald. 208pp. 28999-0

"THE DIAMOND AS BIG AS THE RITZ" AND OTHER STORIES, F. Scott Fitzgerald. 29991-0

MADAME BOVARY, Gustave Flaubert. 256pp. 29257-6

THE REVOLT OF "MOTHER" AND OTHER STORIES, Mary E. Wilkins Freeman. 128pp. 40428-5

A ROOM WITH A VIEW, E. M. Forster. 176pp. (Available in U.S. only.) 28467-0

WHERE ANGELS FEAR TO TREAD, E. M. Forster. 128pp. (Available in U.S. only.) 27791-7

THE IMMORALIST, André Gide. 112pp. (Available in U.S. only.) 29237-1

HERLAND, Charlotte Perkins Gilman. 128pp. 40429-3

"THE YELLOW WALLPAPER" AND OTHER STORIES, Charlotte Perkins Gilman. 80pp. 29857-4

THE OVERCOAT AND OTHER STORIES, Nikolai Gogol. 112pp. 27057-2

CHELKASH AND OTHER STORIES, Maxim Gorky. 64pp. 40652-0

GREAT GHOST STORIES, John Grafton (ed.). 112pp. 27270-2

DETECTION BY GASLIGHT, Douglas G. Greene (ed.). 272pp. 29928-7

THE MABINOGION, Lady Charlotte E. Guest. 192pp. 29541-9

"THE FIDDLER OF THE REELS" AND OTHER SHORT STORIES, Thomas Hardy. 80pp. 29960-0

THE LUCK OF ROARING CAMP AND OTHER STORIES, Bret Harte. 96pp. 27271-0

THE HOUSE OF THE SEVEN GABLES, Nathaniel Hawthorne. 272pp. 40882-5

THE SCARLET LETTER, Nathaniel Hawthorne. 192pp. 28048-9

YOUNG GOODMAN BROWN AND OTHER STORIES, Nathaniel Hawthorne. 128pp. 27060-2

THE GIFT OF THE MAGI AND OTHER SHORT STORIES, O. Henry. 96pp. 27061-0

THE NUTCRACKER AND THE GOLDEN POT, E. T. A. Hoffmann. 128pp. 27806-9

THE BEAST IN THE JUNGLE AND OTHER STORIES, Henry James. 128pp. 27552-3

DAISY MILLER, Henry James. 64pp. 28773-4

THE TURN OF THE SCREW, Henry James. 96pp. 26684-2

WASHINGTON SQUARE, Henry James. 176pp. 40431-5

THE COUNTRY OF THE POINTED FIRS, Sarah Orne Jewett. 96pp. 28196-5

THE AUTOBIOGRAPHY OF AN EX-COLORED MAN, James Weldon Johnson. 112pp. 28512-X

DUBLINERS, James Joyce. 160pp. 26870-5

A PORTRAIT OF THE ARTIST AS A YOUNG MAN, James Joyce. 192pp. 28050-0

THE METAMORPHOSIS AND OTHER STORIES, Franz Kafka. 96pp. 29030-1

THE MAN WHO WOULD BE KING AND OTHER STORIES, Rudyard Kipling. 128pp. 28051-9

YOU KNOW ME AL, Ring Lardner. 128pp. 28513-8

SELECTED SHORT STORIES, D. H. Lawrence. 128pp. 27794-1

GREEN TEA AND OTHER GHOST STORIES, J. Sheridan LeFanu. 96pp. 27795-X

THE CALL OF THE WILD, Jack London. 64pp. 26472-6

FIVE GREAT SHORT STORIES, Jack London. 96pp. 27063-7

THE SEA-WOLF, Jack London. iv+244pp. 41108-7

WHITE FANG, Jack London. 160pp. 26968-X

DEATH IN VENICE, Thomas Mann. 96pp. (Available in U.S. only.) 28714-9

IN A GERMAN PENSION: 13 Stories, Katherine Mansfield. 112pp. 28719-X

DOVER · THRIFT · EDITIONS

FICTION

THE NECKLACE AND OTHER SHORT STORIES, Guy de Maupassant. 128pp. 27064-5
BARTLEBY AND BENITO CERENO, Herman Melville. 112pp. 26473-4
THE OIL JAR AND OTHER STORIES, Luigi Pirandello. 96pp. 28459-X
THE GOLD-BUG AND OTHER TALES, Edgar Allan Poe. 128pp. 26875-6
TALES OF TERROR AND DETECTION, Edgar Allan Poe. 96pp. 28744-0
THE QUEEN OF SPADES AND OTHER STORIES, Alexander Pushkin. 128pp. 28054-3
THE STORY OF AN AFRICAN FARM, Olive Schreiner. 256pp. 40165-0
FRANKENSTEIN, Mary Shelley. 176pp. 28211-2
THREE LIVES, Gertrude Stein. 176pp. (Available in U.S. only.) 28059-4
THE STRANGE CASE OF DR. JEKYLL AND MR. HYDE, Robert Louis Stevenson. 64pp.
  26688-5
TREASURE ISLAND, Robert Louis Stevenson. 160pp. 27559-0
GULLIVER'S TRAVELS, Jonathan Swift. 240pp. 29273-8
THE KREUTZER SONATA AND OTHER SHORT STORIES, Leo Tolstoy. 144pp. 27805-0
THE WARDEN, Anthony Trollope. 176pp. 40076-X
FIRST LOVE AND DIARY OF A SUPERFLUOUS MAN, Ivan Turgenev. 96pp. 28775-0
FATHERS AND SONS, Ivan Turgenev. 176pp. 40073-5
ADVENTURES OF HUCKLEBERRY FINN, Mark Twain. 224pp. 28061-6
THE ADVENTURES OF TOM SAWYER, Mark Twain. 192pp. 40077-8
THE MYSTERIOUS STRANGER AND OTHER STORIES, Mark Twain. 128pp. 27069-6
HUMOROUS STORIES AND SKETCHES, Mark Twain. 80pp. 29279-7
AROUND THE WORLD IN EIGHTY DAYS, Jules Verne. 160pp. 41111-7
CANDIDE, Voltaire (François-Marie Arouet). 112pp. 26689-3
GREAT SHORT STORIES BY AMERICAN WOMEN, Candace Ward (ed.). 192pp. 28776-9
"THE COUNTRY OF THE BLIND" AND OTHER SCIENCE-FICTION STORIES, H. G. Wells. 160pp.
  (Available in U.S. only.) 29569-9
THE ISLAND OF DR. MOREAU, H. G. Wells. 112pp. (Available in U.S. only.) 29027-1
THE INVISIBLE MAN, H. G. Wells. 112pp. (Available in U.S. only.) 27071-8
THE TIME MACHINE, H. G. Wells. 80pp. (Available in U.S. only.) 28472-7
THE WAR OF THE WORLDS, H. G. Wells. 160pp. (Available in U.S. only.) 29506-0
ETHAN FROME, Edith Wharton. 96pp. 26690-7
SHORT STORIES, Edith Wharton. 128pp. 28235-X
THE AGE OF INNOCENCE, Edith Wharton. 288pp. 29803-5
THE PICTURE OF DORIAN GRAY, Oscar Wilde. 192pp. 27807-7
JACOB'S ROOM, Virginia Woolf. 144pp. (Available in U.S. only.) 40109-X
MONDAY OR TUESDAY: Eight Stories, Virginia Woolf. 64pp. (Available in U.S. only.) 29453-6

NONFICTION

POETICS, Aristotle. 64pp. 29577-X
POLITICS, Aristotle. 368pp. 41424-8
NICOMACHEAN ETHICS, Aristotle. 256pp. 40096-4
MEDITATIONS, Marcus Aurelius. 128pp. 29823-X
THE LAND OF LITTLE RAIN, Mary Austin. 96pp. 29037-9
THE DEVIL'S DICTIONARY, Ambrose Bierce. 144pp. 27542-6
THE ANALECTS, Confucius. 128pp. 28484-0
CONFESSIONS OF AN ENGLISH OPIUM EATER, Thomas De Quincey. 80pp. 28742-4
NARRATIVE OF THE LIFE OF FREDERICK DOUGLASS, Frederick Douglass. 96pp. 28499-9

DOVER·THRIFT·EDITIONS

NONFICTION

THE SOULS OF BLACK FOLK, W. E. B. Du Bois. 176pp. 28041-1

SELF-RELIANCE AND OTHER ESSAYS, Ralph Waldo Emerson. 128pp. 27790-9

THE LIFE OF OLAUDAH EQUIANO, OR GUSTAVUS VASSA, THE AFRICAN, Olaudah Equiano. 192pp. 40661-X

THE AUTOBIOGRAPHY OF BENJAMIN FRANKLIN, Benjamin Franklin. 144pp. 29073-5

TOTEM AND TABOO, Sigmund Freud. 176pp. (Available in U.S. only.) 40434-X

LOVE: A Book of Quotations, Herb Galewitz (ed.). 64pp. 40004-2

PRAGMATISM, William James. 128pp. 28270-8

THE STORY OF MY LIFE, Helen Keller. 80pp. 29249-5

TAO TE CHING, Lao Tze. 112pp. 29792-6

GREAT SPEECHES, Abraham Lincoln. 112pp. 26872-1

THE PRINCE, Niccolò Machiavelli. 80pp. 27274-5

THE SUBJECTION OF WOMEN, John Stuart Mill. 112pp. 29601-6

SELECTED ESSAYS, Michel de Montaigne. 96pp. 29109-X

UTOPIA, Sir Thomas More. 96pp. 29583-4

BEYOND GOOD AND EVIL: Prelude to a Philosophy of the Future, Friedrich Nietzsche. 176pp. 29868-X

THE BIRTH OF TRAGEDY, Friedrich Nietzsche. 96pp. 28515-4

COMMON SENSE, Thomas Paine. 64pp. 29602-4

SYMPOSIUM AND PHAEDRUS, Plato. 96pp. 27798-4

THE TRIAL AND DEATH OF SOCRATES: Four Dialogues, Plato. 128pp. 27066-1

A MODEST PROPOSAL AND OTHER SATIRICAL WORKS, Jonathan Swift. 64pp. 28759-9

CIVIL DISOBEDIENCE AND OTHER ESSAYS, Henry David Thoreau. 96pp. 27563-9

SELECTIONS FROM THE JOURNALS (Edited by Walter Harding), Henry David Thoreau. 96pp. 28760-2

WALDEN; OR, LIFE IN THE WOODS, Henry David Thoreau. 224pp. 28495-6

NARRATIVE OF SOJOURNER TRUTH, Sojourner Truth. 80pp. 29899-X

THE THEORY OF THE LEISURE CLASS, Thorstein Veblen. 256pp. 28062-4

DE PROFUNDIS, Oscar Wilde. 64pp. 29308-4

OSCAR WILDE'S WIT AND WISDOM: A Book of Quotations, Oscar Wilde. 64pp. 40146-4

UP FROM SLAVERY, Booker T. Washington. 160pp. 28738-6

A VINDICATION OF THE RIGHTS OF WOMAN, Mary Wollstonecraft. 224pp. 29036-0

PLAYS

PROMETHEUS BOUND, Aeschylus. 64pp. 28762-9

THE ORESTEIA TRILOGY: Agamemnon, The Libation-Bearers and The Furies, Aeschylus. 160pp. 29242-8

LYSISTRATA, Aristophanes. 64pp. 28225-2

WHAT EVERY WOMAN KNOWS, James Barrie. 80pp. (Available in U.S. only.) 29578-8

THE CHERRY ORCHARD, Anton Chekhov. 64pp. 26682-6

THE SEA GULL, Anton Chekhov. 64pp. 40656-3

THE THREE SISTERS, Anton Chekhov. 64pp. 27544-2

UNCLE VANYA, Anton Chekhov. 64pp. 40159-6

THE WAY OF THE WORLD, William Congreve. 80pp. 27787-9

BACCHAE, Euripides. 64pp. 29580-X

MEDEA, Euripides. 64pp. 27548-5

THE MIKADO, William Schwenck Gilbert. 64pp. 27268-0